HOPE'S GIFT

KELLY STARLING LYONS

illustrated by DON TATE

G. P. PUTNAM'S SONS

AN IMPRINT OF PENGUIN GROUP (USA) INC.

For my family and friends,
with thanks and love. —*K. S. L.*

To school librarians everywhere. —*D. T.*

G. P. PUTNAM'S SONS
A division of Penguin Young Readers Group.
Published by The Penguin Group. Penguin Group (USA) Inc.,
375 Hudson Street, New York, NY 10014.

Published simultaneously in Canada. Manufactured in China
by South China Printing Co. Ltd. Design and hand lettered title
by Ryan Thomann. Text set in Oldbook. The art was created
with colored pencils and gouache.

Library of Congress Cataloging-in-Publication Data
Lyons, Kelly Starling. Hope's gift / Kelly Starling Lyons ;
illustrated by Don Tate. p. cm. Summary: A runaway
slave during the Civil War, Hope's father returns after the
Emancipation Proclamation as a member of the U.S. Colored
Troops. [1. African Americans—Fiction. 2. Slavery—Fiction.
3. Emancipation Proclamation—Fiction. 4. Lincoln, Abraham,
1809–1865—Fiction. 5. United States—History—Civil War,
1861–1865—Fiction.] I. Tate, Don, ill. II. Title.
PZ7.L995545Hop 2012 [E]—dc23 2012014587

ISBN 978-0-399-16001-1
10 9 8 7 6 5 4 3 2 1

ALWAYS LEARNING   PEARSON

Christmas night in our cabin, Papa kneeled and wiped the tears from my eyes.

"Saying good-bye," he whispered, "is something you never get used to, even when you're grown."

Papa's eyes got watery as he gazed from me to my little brother, Henry. Mama held her hands over her mouth and turned away. I knew she was hurting too.

"One day, we won't have to be apart," Papa said, hugging me and Henry close. "One day, we'll be free. Maybe this war will make that one day come a little faster."

"But what if . . ." I stopped, scared to ask what would happen if Papa got caught running away.

"Hush," he said, and pulled out a conch shell crowned with spirals.

"Got this when Master hired me out to work on the coast," he said. "Just listen."

Swoosh. Swoosh. A song called out to me.

"That's the sound of freedom, Hope," he said. "And nothing can keep it from coming. Nothing."

"I'll be back as soon as I can," Papa said, kissing Mama and looking at us one last time. Then he slipped into the night.

Me and Henry watched through our cabin window until Papa disappeared. All I saw were woods, looking as lonesome as I felt. As I lay down and closed my eyes, I listened to my shell—*swoosh, swoosh*—and Papa's words rang in my ears.

"Nothing can keep freedom from coming," I whispered. "Nothing."

Master hollered something awful when the holiday times
ended and he learned Papa got away. Said when he finds him,
Papa gonna wish he never got that fool notion to run.

Week after week, Henry hardly said a thing. He carried the clay marbles Papa made him everywhere he went. It was like the outside part of him was there, but something deep inside was gone.

"Papa's gonna come for us," I whispered to him. "Papa's gonna come and we're gonna be a family again."

But some nights, cannons roared and Papa felt farther away than ever. On those nights, me, Mama and Henry huddled together and prayed extra hard that he was okay. On those nights, I listened to my shell—*swoosh, swoosh*—and let its song of freedom take me away.

Sometimes Mama got a piece of news about the war in the cotton field. Sometimes we got it together at prayer meetings deep in the woods.

"Slaves running, swimming, trying to make it to Union lines any way they can," said Ivey, Master's carriage driver. "People say the war worse than anything you ever seen. Both sides suffering. May God help us all."

I looked up at the stars and wondered if Papa was looking up at them too. Was he scared? Was he safe? Could he feel us missing him?

As the war pushed into summer and fall, times got leaner, and Master needed more hands for picking. Instead of helping mind Henry and the other little ones, I started working alongside Mama.

From pink light to purple dark, I picked cotton. At night, Mama nursed my pricks from the burs and told me to hold on. We prayed for Papa and freedom each night before sleep.

One fall morning, Ivey's wife, Viney, leaned close.

"President Lincoln say he gonna free the slaves on New Year's," she whispered with a smile.

My heart jumped as I whispered it to Mama. She grinned and passed it on down the line. I knew she was thinking about Papa, just like me.

That afternoon, Master called everyone to the Big House. He said he was joining the fight. "That scoundrel Lincoln has to be stopped."

His girl, Little Miss, cried and hung on to his neck as tight as she could. As I looked at her, I thought about how I missed Papa's smell—kinda like pine, kinda like sweet earth. I thought about how I missed his big smile that made everything seem brighter. I knew how bad she hurt.

At Christmas, when we sang carols at the Big House, I remembered
Papa's rumbling voice that carried clean across the field. Sadness swept
over me as I thought about the year that passed with him being gone.

Mama wrapped me and Henry in her arms and said to have faith.
Important news was coming. I wondered if the day Papa talked
about was finally here: Would President Lincoln set us free?

Late on New Year's Eve, we gathered in the woods
to pray that President Lincoln would keep his promise.
Just after midnight, Ivey rushed into the clearing.

"The hour is here!" he shouted. "Today Lincoln
gonna set freedom into motion. Won't be long before
we free as any man."

The pat of hands clapping and feet stomping echoed
through the woods. Viney started singing "Now Let Me
Fly." As I danced and sang along, I thought about Papa
coming for us and felt like I had wings.

But after New Year's, it was right back to work. Before I left the quarters, Henry tugged at my arm crying. "I thought we was free," he said.

I wanted to cry too, but I remembered Papa's words.

"Hush," I said, and wiped Henry's tears. "You want to hear something?"

I held my shell to his ear. *Swoosh. Swoosh.*

"That's the sound of freedom, Henry," I said. "And nothing can keep it from coming. Nothing."

Days of waiting turned into weeks and months. Planting season. Still no Papa. When worries hurt my stomach, I listened to my shell and heard Papa's voice in the swooshing.

Picking time came and another lonely Christmas passed. Then, on a spring morning, I looked to the road and saw a troop of colored soldiers wearing Union blue.

One broke into a grin that could outshine the sun. He held his head a bit higher than I remembered. But his eyes were soft and full of tears. "Papa! Papa!" I hollered.

We raced to each other. Papa kissed my cheeks and spun me all around. Then, he grabbed on to Mama and kept on holding like he'd never let go.

"We're free!" Papa shouted. "Free! Go on and get your brother, girl. As many as want to can come along."

News spread in a flash. Ivey and Viney raised their hands to heaven. Everywhere, people hugged and tears streamed down their faces.

When Henry saw Papa, he grinned and held out his marbles.
Papa rubbed Henry's head, then clutched him tight.

In the cabin, as we gathered our things, I thought about all of the people still waiting to be free. I knew their day would come too.

As we left, I took one last look at our past. Then, the wind kissed my cheeks—*swoosh, swoosh*—and the song in my heart made me smile.

"Nothing can keep freedom from coming," I sang. "Nothing."

AUTHOR'S NOTE

On January 1, 1863, President Abraham Lincoln signed the Emancipation Proclamation. That historic document did not abolish slavery, but it gave those enslaved hope and transformed the Civil War into a fight to free slaves as well as one meant to save the Union. Enslaved people were determined to be free. Throughout the war, they fled behind Union lines to places like New Bern, North Carolina. They prayed for deliverance. They served as spies and scouts. Later, free blacks and freedmen also served bravely as soldiers and even liberated people held in bondage on plantations.

When freedom came, many people left plantations to seek out a new life and/or find loved ones. Some made arrangements with former slave owners to receive pay for their work or stayed close by.

More than two years after the Emancipation Proclamation, the Thirteenth Amendment to the U.S. Constitution, which ended slavery, was adopted. A new day was finally here.

I am deeply grateful to Earl Ijames of the North Carolina Museum of History, Gregory Tyler of Historic Hope Plantation, Kimberly Puryear of Historic Stagville, and Dr. Pauletta Bracy for their invaluable help.